© 1994, Editorial LIBSA
  Published by GRANGE BOOKS,
  an imprint of Grange Books plc
  The Grange, Grange Yard
  London SE1 3AG

Published 1994

Illustrated by: JULIAN JORDAN and EVA LOPEZ

Text by: María de Calonje
Translated by: Carmen Healy
Phototypesetting by: Versal Composición, S.L.
Printed by: Egedsa

ISBN: 1-85627-628-7 Legal Dep.: B 23.717 - 1994

Peter Pan

In the city of London there lived three children, a girl called Wendy, and her brothers Michael and John. Every night before going to sleep, Wendy would tell her younger brothers stories or would read them books. Her favourite story was Peter Pan. Wendy told them that he lived with the fairies and didn't want to grow up.

One day she told them that she had found leaves from a tree on the window-sill and she believed that Peter Pan had left them. He had come to see her and would surely return.

One night when their parents had gone to a party and the children were still awake, a very bright light entered through the window. It was Tinker Bell, a fairy so tiny that you could hardly see her. Almost at the same time Peter Pan appeared looking for his shadow.

"Look Peter, it's there on the wall," said Tinker Bell.

The children watched in amazement as Peter trapped his shadow and started playing with it. They were identical, like two peas in a pod.

Suddenly the shadow escaped again. Peter sat on the floor and began to cry.

Wendy asked Peter Pan where he lived.

"Second on the right, straight ahead, 'til morning," he answered.

"What a funny address," laughed Wendy.

"No, it's not funny" said Peter.

"Well that's not an address to which you'd send a letter!" remarked the girl.

Peter told her that he never received letters, not even from his mother. Peter Pan had no parents.

To make Peter happy Wendy sewed his shadow back on and he told them about Never Never Land where the Lost Boys lived.

"Do you want to come with me? I will teach you to fly so that we can get there."

Tinker Bell sprinkled them with a little golden dust and immediately they started to fly.

"Oh, how fantastic!" Michael shouted joyfully flying through the air.

"Let's go to Never Never Land! You'll like it! There are many wonderful things: there are mermaids, Sioux Indians and pirates — a lot of pirates", Peter told them.

"Let's go at once," exclaimed John.

"Let's go at once," repeated Peter and he took off flying very high into the sky, followed by Wendy, Michael, John and Tinker Bell.

They flew and flew for a long time and, at last, they reached an island.

"Look, there's a pirate ship. It's Captain Hook's ship. They call him that because he has a steel hook instead of his right hand."

"A hook?" asked Michael, frightened.

"Yes, a long time ago a big crocodile bit off his hand, watch and all, and now the crocodile wants to eat him whole. When the Captain hears the tick-tock of the watch, he knows the crocodile is near and he is terrified."

Tinker Bell began to be jealous of Wendy because Peter paid so much attention to her. She rushed passed everyone and quickly flew down to look for the Lost Boys who were playing with bows and arrows.

"Quick boys, Peter wants you to shoot that bird that is flying with him."

One of them shot an arrow that struck Wendy's chest and she feel to the ground.

When the Lost Boys saw that they had shot a girl and not a bird, they felt scared and guilty. Peter was angry with Tinker Bell and pushed her aside.

Suddenly Wendy stood up. The arrow had become stuck in a button on her dress. The jolt had thrown her to the ground but she was only a little shaken.

The lost boys immediately began to build a small house for Wendy. Because they all helped, the house was soon finished.

Wendy took care of Peter, her brothers and the Lost Boys. At night she told them stories and sang lovely songs.

Captain Hook had kidnapped the Big Sioux Chief's daughter, Princess Tiger Lily. When Peter heard, he made plans to rescue her. He went to look for Hook and bravely confronted him. Though wounded by the terrible hook, Peter freed young Tiger Lily and flew off with her to her father's camp.

Wendy and her brothers thought of returning home. Their parents would worry if they couldn't find them upon returning from the party. When they were ready to leave, the children were attacked by pirates. They fought bravely, but there were many attackers and Wendy and the boys were held prisoner and taken to the pirate ship.

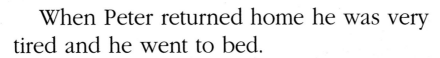

When Peter returned home he was very
tired and he went to bed.

Captain Hook who had followed him,
seeing him asleep, decided to get revenge.

He poured some drops of a powerful
poison in Peter Pan's cup and silently left.

The next day, when Peter awoke he took the cup ready to drink.

"Don't drink! It's poisoned," shouted Tinker Bell, who had returned full of regret.

"Don't lie," said Peter and began to drink.

The determined fairy got between the cup and his lips spilling the poisoned liquid. Unfortunately a couple of drops fell in her mouth and at once her little wings could no longer hold her up and she fell to the ground.

"I'm going to die," whispered Tinker Bell. "But I could be saved if all children believed in fairies."

Peter stretched out his arms and shouted, "If you believe in fairies, clap with all your might and you can save Tinker Bell."

Suddenly the fairy's wings began to flutter and a few seconds later she was flying about.

Wendy was tied to the large mast on the pirate ship and the boys were about to be thrown overboard.

When they began walking the plank that would take them to certain death, something terrible could be heard: the tick-tock from the crocodile that wanted to eat Captain Hook.

"Hide me, help me," screamed Captain Hook scared to death.

He hadn't realised that Peter was making the noise.

Suddenly the ticking stopped. That gave the pirate courage who then shouted furiously for the boys to be thrown in the sea.

"No boy will be thrown overboard," said Peter while jumping onto the ship's deck.

They began to fight. Peter was a very good swordsman, but so was Captain Hook. The fight was just between the two of them.

One attacked, the other defended himself, back and forth. But no one else joined in.

When Hook went in for the final blow, Peter managed to avoid him and with a strong push sent him flying off the ship. Now the crocodile was really waiting for him in the water.

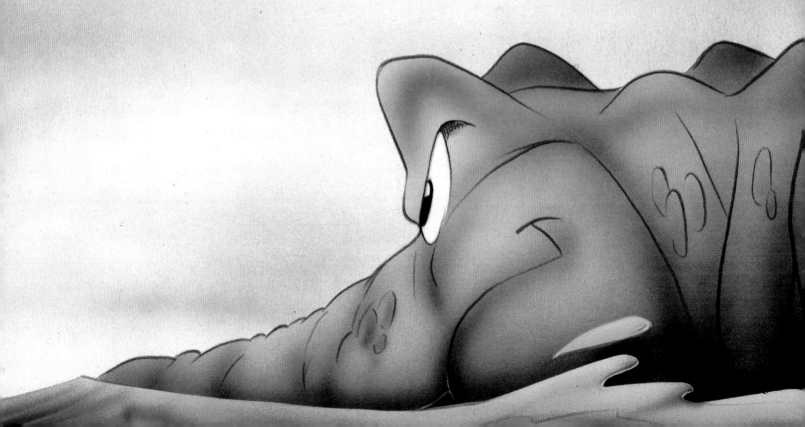

Swimming as fast as he could, Captain
Hook tried to escape the terrible crocodile
that followed him with hungry eyes.

Without a captain, the pirates were confused and, although there were many, no one knew what to do. With Peter's help, the boys threw some of them overboard, other jumped by themselves. All at once, the sea was full of pirates.

In London, Wendy, Michael and John's parents were very worried and missed their children, but Peter didn't want them to return. He wanted them to stay with him forever in Never Never Land. He sent Tinker Bell to close the children's window, hoping that when they saw it closed, they would think their parents no longer loved them. Then they would stay with him.

But when they reached the house and Peter saw that the parents were so upset, he opened the window to let them in. The three children were very happy. Back in their room, they got straight into bed.

"Do you want to stay here and live with us?" they asked him.

43

"Go to school, grow up, become a man, have worries and problems? No, no one will get me to grow up!" said Peter convinced and he flew away in the starry night back to Never Never Land.